Welcome to ALADDIN QUIX!

If you are looking for fast, fun-to-read stories with colorful characters, lots of kid-friendly humor, easy-to-follow action, entertaining story lines, and lively illustrations, then **ALADDIN QUIX** is for you!

But wait, there's more!

If you're also looking for stories with tables of contents; word lists; about-the-book questions; 64, 80, or 96 pages; short chapters; short paragraphs; and large fonts, then **ALADDIN QUIX** is *definitely* for you!

ALADDIN QUIX: The next step between ready to reads and longer, more challenging chapter books, for readers five to eight years old.

Read more ALADDIN QUIX books!

A Miss Mallard Mystery
By Robert Quackenbush

A Miss Mallard Mystery

RICKSHAW TO HORROR

ROBERT QUACKENBUSH

ALADDIN QUIX

New York London Toronto Sydney New Delhi

ALADDIN QUIX

Simon & Schuster Children's Publishing Division

1230 Avenue of the Americas, New York, New York 10020

First Aladdin QUIX hardcover edition September 2022

Copyright © 1984 by Robert Quackenbush

Also available in an Aladdin QUIX paperback edition.

All rights reserved, including the right of reproduction in whole or in part in any form.

ALADDIN and the related marks and colophon are trademarks of Simon & Schuster, Inc.

For information about special discounts for bulk purchases, please contact Simon & Schuster Special Sales at 1-866-506-1949 or business@simonandschuster.com.

The Simon & Schuster Speakers Bureau can bring authors to your live event. For more information or to book an event contact the Simon & Schuster Speakers Bureau at 1-866-248-3049 or visit our website at www.simonspeakers.com.

Designed by Tiara Iandiorio

The illustrations for this book were rendered in pen and ink and wash.

The text of this book was set in Archer Medium.

Manufactured in the United States of America 0822 LAK

2 4 6 8 10 9 7 5 3 1

Library of Congress Control Number 2022936585

ISBN 9781534413191 (hc)

ISBN 9781534413184 (pbk)

ISBN 9781534413207 (ebook)

For Piet

Cast of Characters

Miss Mallard: World-famous ducktective

Lee Duck: Rickshaw driver

Marshall Gadwall: Retired navy captain

Officer Pintail: Police officer in Hong Kong

Harold: Valet to Marshall and Melissa Gadwall

Melissa Gadwall: Married to Marshall Gadwall

What's in Miss Mallard's Bag?

Miss Mallard has many detective tools she brings with her on her adventures around the world.

In her knitting bag she usually has:

- Newspaper clippings
- Knitting needles and yarn
- A magnifying glass
- A flashlight
- A mirror
- A travel guide
- Chocolates for her nephew

Contents

1

Dragon Festival

All of Hong Kong was celebrating the Dragon Boat Festival. Boat-racing teams had come from every corner, all over the world.

It was a sight to see!

On one street, a Dragon Dance went weaving back and forth through the crowd. Suddenly, a **rickshaw** raced ahead of the dragon.

"Lee Duck!" cried **Miss Mallard**, the world-famous duck-tective. **"Please slow down!** You're going much too fast! How can I see the sights of Hong Kong at this speed?"

"Sorry," said Lee Duck.

Lee Duck quickly turned a cor-ner onto a quieter street. At the

same moment, someone stepped off the sidewalk and was knocked down by the rickshaw.

"Horrors!" cried Miss Mallard. "We hit someone!"

Lee Duck stopped the rickshaw. Miss Mallard jumped out and looked under it as a police officer came running over.

"Are you all right under there?" called Miss Mallard. "I'm Margery Mallard. I've seen you before. We're staying at the same hotel. I'm terribly sorry about this."

"**Marshall Gadwall**, retired navy captain, here," quacked a **feeble** voice. "I'm fine. Just a bit dizzy from hitting my head."

Gadwall crawled out from under the rickshaw. He looked dazed.

"Perhaps you should see a doctor," said the police officer.

"No, no," said Gadwall. "I am quite all right. Besides, this is Sunday, and it is nearly eleven o'clock. I must be off to an important appointment."

"But today is Saturday," said Miss Mallard.

"No, Sunday," said Gadwall. "Don't you remember? At this same hour yesterday—Saturday—someone raised a **typhoon** warning flag at the ferry **terminal**. All the ferries stopped running, and everyone rushed for shelter."

The police officer said, "I'll prove to you that today is Saturday."

He called someone on his walkie-talkie. When he finished, he looked at Gadwall.

"Great Dragons!" he said. "Someone *did* raise a false warning flag at the terminal just now. The crowd is in a panic, and the police are trying to sort things out. But how could you **predict** it? It must be a **coincidence**. You had better go to your hotel now. I'm **Officer Pintail**, if you should need me again."

"I'll take Captain Gadwall to the hotel," said Miss Mallard. "It's just around the corner."

2

Teatime

As they were walking to the hotel, Gadwall decided to have some tea. He asked Miss Mallard to join him.

"I never could turn down a cup of tea," said Miss Mallard.

"Good!" said Gadwall. "I'll meet you in the lounge. I must send my **valet**, **Harold**, on an errand. My wife, **Melissa**, is shopping and should return soon. I'd like you two to meet."

Miss Mallard went into the lounge, and sat at a table by the window facing the lobby.

She took a travel guidebook from her knitting bag and began to read. The book said that a million-dollar jade necklace was on **display** at the Duckworth Museum.

I'd like to see that, she thought.

Miss Mallard looked up and saw Gadwall talking to Harold, who was wearing a gray valet's jacket. Then Harold left, and Mrs. Gadwall came into the hotel. Gadwall brought his wife into the lounge.

"I'm pleased to meet you," said Melissa Gadwall. "Are you here for the Dragon Boat Festival?"

"Yes," said Miss Mallard. "Are you?"

"I prefer shopping," said

Melissa Gadwall. "Especially for jade."

Marshall Gadwall cleared his throat and changed the subject. He told his wife about the accident.

"And the strangest thing, dear!" Gadwall said. "When I was hit on the head, I could predict things."

"Like what?" asked his wife.

Suddenly Gadwall turned very silent. He looked at his watch. Then he looked at Miss Mallard.

"What's wrong?" asked Miss Mallard.

"In exactly five minutes," said Gadwall, "it will be twelve o'clock. That's when someone will cut the ropes of the famous Peeking Duck Floating Restaurant and set it **adrift** in the harbor."

Miss Mallard gasped!

She quickly got up from the table.

"What is this about?" **pleaded** Melissa Gadwall.

"It is another of your husband's predictions!" said Miss Mallard. "Wait here. **I'll notify the police!**"

3

Peeking Duck

Miss Mallard ran outside. She saw Lee Duck and waved to him. He rushed over with his rickshaw, and Miss Mallard climbed in.

"Take me to Officer Pintail!" said Miss Mallard.

"And Lee, this time you can hurry!"

They found Officer Pintail on a side street. Miss Mallard told him about the new prediction.

"I'll check it out," said Officer Pintail. "The restaurant is only a few blocks away."

They all rushed to the waterfront. When they got there, the Peeking Duck Floating Restaurant had been cut loose from its ropes. It was drifting out to sea. Everyone on board was quacking loudly

to be rescued. Office Pintail called for help on his walkie-talkie.

In a flash, fire trucks and police cars came racing to the waterfront. At the same time, out in the harbor, rescue boats were at work, pushing the restaurant back to shore.

When the floating restaurant was safe, Office Pintail filled out a report. The restaurant manager said he did not know who had cut the ropes. He asked who had sounded the alarm.

"I did," said Miss Mallard.

"Thank you," said the manager. "Please be our guest for dinner anytime."

"Actually," said Miss Mallard, "someone at my hotel, Marshall Gadwall, warned me that you were in danger."

"Really? Please invite him to dinner too," said the manager.

Then Miss Mallard went looking for Lee Duck. On the way, she saw a gray thread dangling from one of the cut ropes of the floating restaurant.

She looked at the thread with her magnifying glass.

"Hmmmm," she said.

Then she put it between the pages of her travel guidebook and put the book back in her knitting bag. Afterward, she found Lee Duck and rode away in his rickshaw.

4

Another Prediction

As the rickshaw sped through the streets, Miss Mallard couldn't stop thinking about the gray thread she had discovered.

When they arrived at the hotel, she thanked Lee Duck and ran inside. She found Gadwall alone in the lounge.

He said that Mrs. Gadwall had gone shopping again. Miss Mallard told him how his second prediction had come true. Someone had cut the ropes to the floating restaurant.

She also told him about the manager's dinner invitation.

"That was nice of him," said Gadwell. "But I won't be able to go. Floating restaurants make me **seasick**."

Just then, Officer Pintail arrived. He needed some information for his report on the restaurant. He asked Gadwall how he was able to predict bad events.

"I have no idea," said Gadwall. "Ever since the rickshaw accident, pictures just seem to pop into my head."

Suddenly he stopped talking and looked at his watch.

"What is it?" asked Miss Mallard.

Gadwall answered, "In five

minutes, it will be exactly three o'clock. That's when someone will let the air out of the tires of all the tour buses at the Victoria Bazaar. There will be a major traffic jam."

Officer Pintail was **alarmed**.

"Wait here!" he said to Gadwall as he ran from the hotel.

Miss Mallard ran too. She hired Lee Duck to take her to the **bazaar**. When she got there, she saw all the flat tires and the major traffic jam that Gadwall had described. Ducks were quacking their heads off. Just as before, the police could not find out who had done it.

It was hours before the tires were fixed and the police **unsnarled** the traffic. All the while, Miss Mallard kept looking for clues. But she found nothing.

Finally Lee Duck took her back to the hotel. When she got there, she saw many reporters **crowding** around the front entrance.

"Horrors!" Miss Mallard said aloud. "The news is out about Gadwall's predictions."

5

Zounds!

Miss Mallard squeezed past the reporters and went into the hotel. She saw Officer Pintail and the police chief **questioning** Gadwall in the lounge.

"I know what I know," Gadwall

was saying. "Tomorrow morning at exactly ten o'clock, during the boat races, some of the boats will be destroyed. A **riot** will break out, and the Dragon Boat Festival will end in disaster."

"We must **prevent** that from happening," said Officer Pintail.

"I'll send a large police force to the races in the morning," said the chief.

Miss Mallard was **puzzled**. Why did all of Gadwall's predictions involve the police? She excused herself and went to her room. It had been an **exhausting** day, and she needed to be alone so she could think.

She ordered supper in her room. All evening she went over and over the events of the day.

Miss Mallard thought about her only clue, the gray thread, which she had placed in her travel guidebook.

But no matter how much she thought, she was still as puzzled as ever.

At bedtime, she opened the book and saw the thread was still there. She closed the book again and stared at it. Then she put it away and went to sleep.

When Miss Mallard awoke the next morning, it was already nine o'clock. And Gadwall's prediction was set for ten!

Miss Mallard **bounded** out of bed. And suddenly everything was clear to her! She grabbed her knitting bag. She reached inside and gave her travel guidebook a pat.

Then she dug through her clipping file for a **particular** news item.

"Zounds!" she said when she found it.

Quickly she got dressed and ran to the front desk. She asked where she could find the Gadwalls.

"Sorry," said the clerk. "They checked out this morning."

"I thought so!" said Miss Mallard. She rushed outside.

"Quick!" she cried to Lee Duck. "Take me to Officer Pintail."

When they found Officer Pintail, Miss Mallard said, "It's about the Gadwalls! They left the hotel! At this very moment, I believe they are stealing the million-dollar jade necklace on display at the Duckworth Museum! The accident and predictions were **faked**! The Gadwalls planned to keep the police busy so the museum would be less protected against robbery!"

"Great Dragons!" said Officer Pintail. "I'll send a police car to the museum right away!"

6

Jade-Handed

Lee Duck sped with Miss Mallard to the museum. Officer Pintail and the other police were already there. They were crowded around the museum's side entrance.

Miss Mallard went over. She

saw Marshall Gadwall, Melissa Gadwall, and Harold, all in handcuffs.

"Well, you were right, Miss Mallard," said Officer Pintail. "We caught them in the act, just as they were coming out the door with the necklace."

"How did you know we would be here?" **grumbled** Marshall Gadwall.

"Thanks to my travel guidebook," said Miss Mallard. "I saw a picture of the jade necklace in it,

and I remembered that your wife said she was 'shopping' for jade. I also remembered that you said you were a retired navy captain. Since when do navy captains get seasick on floating restaurants? Then all it took was a look in my clipping file to find out your true identity—'Slippery' Gadwall, the well-known thief and swindler."

Miss Mallard paused and reached into her knitting bag. She pulled out the gray thread.

"Here is a thread that I found

at the floating restaurant," said Miss Mallard. "As you can see, it matches Harold's jacket. Not only that—you claimed that your wife had gone shopping yesterday morning. And yet she returned to the hotel empty-handed. I believe that you sent your wife and Harold out to cause the events that you 'predicted.' And you followed me to fake the rickshaw accident, knowing that I would get the police involved. It was all a **scheme** to fool the police, so the museum would be less protected while you robbed it."

"Take them away," said Officer Pintail to the squad. "I'll tell the chief that there will be no trouble at the Dragon Boat races."

Then Officer Pintail turned to Miss Mallard and said, **"Good job!"**

"Well, I'm glad we saved the necklace," said Miss Mallard. "The Gadwalls had me fooled for a while."

Lee Duck said, "How about

seeing the sights of Hong Kong now—very slowly?"

"Why, Lee!" said Miss Mallard. **"What a good idea!"**

Word List

adrift (uh·DRIFT): Floating or moving without being steered

alarmed (uh·LAHRMD): Very worried or surprised

bazaar (buh·ZAHR): An outdoor street market where people buy and sell goods

bounded (BOWN·did): Leaped up

coincidence (co·IN·sih·dens): The chance of two things happening at the same time

crowding (CRAHW·ding):
Packing tightly in a small space

display (diss·PLAY): Being
shown in public

exhausting (egg·ZAW·sting):
Tiring

faked (FAYKD): Not real or
genuine

feeble (FEE·bull): Weak, not
strong

grumbled (GRUM·buld): Made
deep, angry sounds

particular (pahr·TICK·yoo·luhr):
Chosen for a special reason

pleaded (PLEE·did): Asked for something in a sincere way

predict (pree·DICT): To tell when something in the future will happen

prevent (pree·VENT): Stop from happening

puzzled (PUH·zuld): Confused

questioning (KWES·chun·ing): Asking lots of questions

rickshaw (RIK·shaw): A two-wheeled cart that carries one or two passengers and is pulled by a person

riot (RYE·ut): Public disorder that is often violent

scheme (SKEEM): A crafty plan

seasick (SEE·sick): Feeling nauseous from being on the water

terminal (TUHR·min·ull): A station for buses, ships, or airplanes

typhoon (tie·FOON): A hurricane storm that occurs in the western Pacific Ocean

unsnarled (uhn·SNARLD): Untangled or put back into order

valet (VALL·ay): Someone who is hired to help run personal errands

Questions

1. What color was the thread Miss Mallard found? Where did she find it?
2. What did Melissa Gadwall like shopping for?
3. Marshall Gadwall retired from doing what?
4. Why was Miss Mallard telling Lee Duck to slow down in the rickshaw? Did anything happen when he raced through the streets?

5. Why did Gadwall say he couldn't go to the Peeking Duck Floating Restaurant?

CHUCKLE YOUR WAY THROUGH THESE EASY-TO-READ ILLUSTRATED CHAPTER BOOKS!